READ ALL OF
AXEL & BEAST'S
ADVENTURES!

First American Edition 2019
Kane Miller, A Division of EDC Publishing

Text copyright © 2017 Adrian C. Bott
Illustrations copyright © 2017 Andy Issac
First published in Australia by Hardie Grant Egmont

For information contact:
Kane Miller, A Division of EDC Publishing
PO Box 470663
Tulsa, OK 74147-0663
www.kanemiller.com
www.edcpub.com
www.usbornebooksandmore.com

Library of Congress Control Number: 2018942397

Printed and bound in the United States of America

2 3 4 5 6 7 8 9 10

ISBN: 978-1-61067-850-6

THE OMEGA OPERATION

ADRIAN C. BOTT ART BY ANDY ISAAC

Kane Miller
A DIVISION OF EDC PUBLISHING

CHAPTER 1

Axel's best friend, BEAST, was a robot.

Most of the time BEAST was roughly person shaped, with a head and arms and legs. But if he had the right app installed in his memory, BEAST could **shape-shift** into other forms, like his Antarctic explorer form, SNOWDOG, or his knight-in-armor battle form, GALAHAD. Each form had its own special strengths and weaknesses, but they all had one thing in common. They were **_exciting_**.

Right now, though, BEAST was in a form so boring Axel thought its app must have been created as a joke. His friend Agent Omega had sent it to him on a USB drive along with half-a-dozen other "wacky" apps because "You never know when something like this might come in useful."

The form was called FRIJ.

It turned BEAST into a refrigerator.

Right now, BEAST was sitting in the dark kitchen, humming to himself, happily being a fridge. He had learned that fridges are supposed to hum, so he was humming a song called "Never Gonna Give You Up" that he had learned from the Internet. Axel had told him fridges don't hum *tunes*, they just hum in a sort of peaceful drone, but BEAST had

already forgotten this.

Meanwhile, over in the living room, Axel was playing on his video game console. Once, he'd played games to hide away from the world. Now, he and his friend Yumi played together online to train for **missions against evil corporations** like Grabbem Industries. Yumi was in Japan, but that didn't matter when you had a fast Internet connection.

Right now, Axel was running away from a teddy bear with a machine gun. The pink, fuzzy bear bellowed a battle cry and blasted a round of **jelly beans** at him.

Axel ducked and rolled, and the jelly beans shot harmlessly overhead. He activated a **speed boost** and charged toward Mushroom Base. He yelled, "Yumi! They're coming!"

Yumi's voice rang out from the speakers: "I've prepared a special welcome. Just stick to the plan! You run around and distract them while I defend the base!"

One of the best things about **Bubble Gum Bear Battle Bonanza** was how many character classes you could choose from. Axel liked to play as a Scout, since they were fast moving and could do acrobatic stunts. Yumi preferred the Tech class, because a Tech could build traps and turrets for enemies to blunder into.

Over a sunny green hill came a crowd of multicolored teddy bears, waving swords, axes and rocket launchers. They were heading for Axel and Yumi's base, which was shaped like a giant red mushroom. If the enemy could kick Yumi out and capture the base for themselves, their team would be certain to win. There were only two minutes left in the game.

Yumi stepped onto Mushroom Base's little wooden balcony. Her bear character was dressed in power armor and carried a toolbox. She crouched down and went into a blur of movement. The next second, a freshly built **Toffee Turret** stood there beside her.

Axel reached the door of Mushroom Base. According to the plan they'd worked out, he was supposed to keep his distance and leave the defending to Yumi. But maybe that wasn't such a good plan. Surely two of them could defend better than one?

The oncoming enemy bears were almost at the door. Axel made up his mind. He ran inside Mushroom Base and got ready to defend.

The door exploded into wafer-like

fragments. The invading horde of Bubble Gum Bears came charging into Mushroom Base.

"Eat **rainbow devastation**, creeps!" yelled Yumi.

The Toffee Turret juddered and swung around. A thunderous volley of shimmering Friendship Jelly Beans blew the floor of Mushroom Base into a cratered ruin. A few of the attacking bears vanished in little explosions of red hearts, overcome by the firepower of concentrated friendship, but most of them were still coming.

Then the entire screen flashed red. A gigantic heart-shaped explosion engulfed Mushroom Base completely.

Axel watched, openmouthed, as the game's defeat counter flashed up the news: every single bear in Mushroom Base had been

knocked out by the blast. Including him and Yumi.

"Yumi, did you just trigger a Love Bomb?"

"Of course!" Yumi laughed. "That was my plan all along!"

"But that knocks **us** out as well as the enemy!"

"Doesn't matter," Yumi said. "So long as one of us survives, we win. And you survived, didn't you?"

"Um," said Axel.

"You kept your distance like we agreed … right?"

"Er," said Axel.

"BOTH TEAMS ELIMINATED. THIS ROUND IS A DRAW," said the robotic announcer.

"I, uh … thought you needed help," said Axel.

"Axel, you *punk!*" Yumi yelled, so loudly that BEAST stopped humming and looked up. "I didn't ask for your help. I was counting on you to **stick to the plan**!"

Axel sighed. Yumi let out an *ooooh* of utter fury.

"I'm sorry," Axel said. "It just didn't seem right to leave you alone."

"You weren't leaving me. I *asked* you to go. Now I'm going to get an experience-point penalty for blowing up my own team member! Axel, we can't fight as a team if you don't do the things you say you're going to do!"

"I said I was sorry!"

"Whatever. Let's take a break. Back in five."

"IS YUMI OKAY?" asked BEAST, as Axel sighed again and leaned back on the couch.

"Yeah. She's just **mad** at me. I don't blame her. I guess I let her down."

BEAST shifted out of FRIJ form into his regular robot shape, shuffled across the room and laid a hand on Axel's shoulder.

"I AM SORRY SHE DID NOT HAVE MORE NEWS FOR YOU."

"Me too," said Axel.

Axel let his mind stray back to the night when Yumi had told him, "We think we know **what happened to your dad**." Crazy to think it was only a week ago.

"He's definitely alive," she'd told him. "And he's being kept prisoner by a powerful group. We don't know which one yet, but it's *not* Grabbem. My mother spotted his name on a partially decoded transmission. Matt Brayburn. Subject 547."

Axel hated that word, *subject*. It made him think of "test subject." The thought that someone could be **doing experiments**

on his dad made him clench his fist until the nails dug into his palm.

When he'd told his mom, she'd cried and laughed and then cried some more. "I knew it," she said. "I always told you, didn't I? He's *alive*. And as soon as Yumi finds out exactly where he is, you and BEAST can bring him back! I'm sure Agent Omega will help, too."

Agent Omega had a job at Grabbem Industries, but he was a double agent, helping Axel to fight them. He usually called every other day to talk about new missions, but he hadn't been in touch all week. Axel was almost relieved about that. How could he concentrate on fighting Grabbem when his dad was being held prisoner somewhere? All he wanted to do was rescue him.

Something at the back of the house went **tap, tap, tap.**

Axel glanced up. Green light was pouring through the rear windows. A **metal tentacle** was tapping on the glass. It dangled from a round, hovering craft. BEAST gasped.

"AXEL, IT IS THE MOT-BOL!"

"You're right! Agent Omega must have flown it here!"

The MOT-BOL, or Meatball as Axel liked to call it, was their home away from home when they were on missions. It was a flying docking station for BEAST to retreat to, so he could recharge and repair himself.

Axel and BEAST ran out into the backyard. The MOT-BOL hovered low, hiding itself behind the trees. It slowly landed in front of them like an **alien spacecraft**.

Axel felt a chill that ran deeper than the cold of the evening. Something was wrong.

He knew it, with that sickly certainty you get when you are sure there's bad news coming, but nobody wants to be the one to tell you.

He called out, "Agent Omega?"

But there was no answer.

The silent craft was completely empty.

CHAPTER 2

Axel slowly crept forward until he could look right up inside the MOT-BOL. There was no sign of Agent Omega. Or anyone else.

BEAST's ears twitched as he picked up a signal. "THE MOT-BOL SAYS IT CAME HERE ON AUTOPILOT. IT HAS A MESSAGE FOR YOUR EARS ONLY," said BEAST. "IT SAYS YOU MUST GO ABOARD."

Axel's skin prickled. *This could be a trap*, he thought. By now, Yumi would be impatiently waiting for the next round of their game. He badly wanted to go back indoors, but this felt deadly serious.

"Should I?" he asked BEAST.

"YES," said BEAST. "THE MOT-BOL IS OUR FRIEND. WE CAN TRUST IT."

Axel climbed up inside the MOT-BOL. A single button was blinking on and off, shining the spooky golden color of a cat's eyes in the dark. He pressed it.

Agent Omega appeared in the air in front of him. **He was transparent and glowing blue.**

Axel jumped. Then he realized this wasn't a ghost. It was a hologram, just like the very first time Agent Omega had spoken to them.

The hologram of Agent Omega glanced over his shoulder. Sweat was beading on his brow.

"Axel, if you're watching this recorded message, it means **the worst has happened**. Listen carefully. My life, and the future of our whole operation, is hanging in the balance."

Axel felt like all the bones had fallen out of his body. Finding out that things were every bit as bad as you had feared was a strange (but somehow horribly satisfying) feeling.

"For some time now," said the hologram, "I've felt like Grabbem were breathing down my neck. Like they were going to find out I'm working with you any second. Then today, these two men in white coats came to check my computer, and they wouldn't say what it was for. Then they checked my pulse rate.

I was so nervous, my heart was thumping. They're onto me. I know it."

"We'll help!" Axel burst out. Then he remembered Agent Omega couldn't hear him.

"My only hope now is you and BEAST. That's why I've set up a special system with the MOT-BOL in case they've caught me. See the keyboard here? Every day, I have to type in a password that only I know. If I ever *don't* put the password in, it means I can't because something's happened to me. In that event, the MOT-BOL is programmed to head directly to you, under cover of darkness."

"Clever system," Axel said.

"Now I need to prep you for the mission I hoped I'd never have to send you on," continued Agent Omega. "The MOT-BOL will fly you and BEAST to Platinum Acres, where the Grabbem family lives. Under their mansion is an enormous underground factory complex. My workplace. I'm somewhere inside it, most likely in a prison cell. Axel, I need you to break in … and break me out."

He pointed to a cable that hung down from the roof. "Plug that into the back of BEAST's neck, and he'll download the apps you need. I've loaded up SKYHAWK, OGRE, MYTHFIRE and a couple of new ones called PILLBUG and SHADO. PILLBUG turns him into an armored form. He can't do anything apart from crawl around and roll into a ball, but he's pretty much impossible to hurt. SHADO is a stealth striker. Almost no armor in that form, but if he keeps still, he's **completely invisible**, and a powerful blade attacks. Use that one to take out sentry drones and stuff. I'm sure you can figure out plenty more uses."

The hologram looked right at Axel. It was spooky, as if it could actually see him.

"I'm counting on you, Axel. You're the only one who can **pull me out of the fire**. Good luck – and thanks."

It disappeared.

Axel climbed back outside and just stood on the grass, thunderstruck. "We're going to break into *Grabbem Headquarters*?" he said.

He and BEAST had gone to some risky places in the past. They'd narrowly escaped from giant metal tentacles in a secret iceberg base, and almost been **stomped flat by a towering robot** in a deserted island city. But now Agent Omega was asking them to go to the most dangerous place in the entire world, for them.

And if I'm scared, Axel thought, *what must poor BEAST be going through? That*

Grabbem factory is where he was made. It's where he ran away from! If they catch him in there, they'll take him to pieces!

Sure enough, BEAST was **trembling** all over.

"BEAST?" said Axel gently.

"I MISS BEING A FRIDGE," said BEAST, in a little voice. "I LIKE BEING A FRIDGE. IT IS SAFE AND BORING AND I CAN TALK TO THE FROZEN PEAS AND NOBODY TRIES TO BLOW ME UP."

"When all this is over and we've beaten Grabbem once and for all, you can be a fridge for as long as you like. I promise," Axel said.

"I DO NOT WANT TO GO BACK THERE!" BEAST wailed. "WHAT IF THEY CAPTURE ME AND ERASE MY MEMORIES AND I FORGET I EVER MET YOU? WHAT IF THEY MAKE ME HURT YOU?"

"That won't happen!"

"AXEL HAS NEVER BEEN INSIDE ... INSIDE THE GRABBEM PLACE. BUT BEAST HAS. **BEAST KNOWS**!"

He can hardly bear to say the word Grabbem out loud, Axel thought. *He's being so brave.*

He tried to think of what to say to comfort BEAST, but he couldn't. The trouble was, BEAST was right. Axel had no idea what the kindly robot had been through in that dreadful place. He wrapped both his arms around BEAST's arm and gave him a hug.

"You're a lot **braver** than you know, mate," he said. "I know you're scared. So am I. But Agent Omega's scared, too. We can't let him down."

They sat like that for several minutes. Neither of them said anything.

Then, very slowly, BEAST straightened up. A look of determination seemed to come over his face. He pulled the USB drive with the FRIJ app on it out of his arm and handed it to Axel. Then he marched up into the MOT-BOL, grabbed the cable and plugged it into his neck.

"RECEIVING DATA!" he announced.

"Wait," Axel said. "Does this mean ..."

"NEW APPS INSTALLED. BEAST IS

READY TO FIGHT."

"BEAST, I need to be a hundred percent clear on this. Are you saying you're coming with me?"

"YES."

Axel grinned. "Way to go! I'd better just go and write a note for Mom, or she'll panic. Then we can go and fetch Agent Omega. Right?"

"RIGHT," said BEAST. "AGENT OMEGA HELPED BEAST ESCAPE GRABBEM. BEAST OWES HIM EVERYTHING. SO IF BEAST CANNOT BE BRAVE ENOUGH TO HELP HIM NOW, THEN ... THEN BEAST MIGHT AS WELL GO AND BE A FRIDGE FOREVER!"

CHAPTER
3

Mr. Gus Grabbem Senior, the head of Grabbem Industries, lay tucked up in a big circular bed. The bedspread was made to look like planet Earth, because Mr. Grabbem liked to imagine that the whole world was his. Sometimes he jumped up and down on it.

He couldn't sleep. He was excited because it was the day before the Big Tour. This was a special event where he took a group of people around his **enormous** factory, so that they would be impressed and invest lots of money in his company. It was important that it went well because the more impressed they were, the more money he stood to get.

He scrolled through his emails on a golden laptop while his wife read *The Endangered Species Cookbook*.

"They're coming," he said, and rubbed his hands with glee. "They can all come!"

"That's great, honey," said Mrs. Grabbem, without looking up.

"Even Lady Porkington-Trotter is flying over from England!"

"Won't that be nice. Are the **Crusherbots** all ready?"

"Oh, yes, my dainty little dollop. We'll show them off as the grand finale."

The Big Tour wasn't just about money. It was about showing off, and the whole point of being rich was that you got to show off. Most people didn't understand that. They thought that being rich was about being able to get what you wanted. But even when you were only a little bit rich, you didn't really *want* anything anymore. You could always buy a meal if you were hungry, or warm yourself up if you were cold. You could see any movie you wanted to see. So when you were ridiculously rich, life was so boring that showing off to other rich people was the only thing left to do.

Apart from give money to charity, of course, but Mr. Grabbem wasn't that kind of person.

Mr. Grabbem looked over the guest list for tomorrow. What an **amazing party** this was going to be. Even Gus Grabbem Junior was going to have fun, playing with the other rich people's kids.

The list read:

- JUSTIN SMOOTHLEY, supermodel, no children, and his chihuahua, LYSANDER.
- HENGIST PUNKERDUNK, oil baron, and his children, EZEKIEL and WANDA.
- LADY FLORA PORKINGTON-

TROTTER, sausage queen, and her daughter, PIPPA.

- JUANITA CASTILLO, art trader, and her daughter, BELLADONNA.
- GENERAL LUCILLE "SPINE-RIPPER" REGAN (retired), and her son, BUCKSHOT.
- PROFESSOR ARNOLD PAYNE, Director of the Neuron Institute, no children.

All the hairs on Mr. Grabbem's back stood on end as he read the words **"Neuron Institute,"** and, just for a second, his good mood wavered.

They were **deeply creepy people**, that group. Professor Payne had a damp, clammy handshake and his face was as waxy white as a **dead crocodile's belly**. Mr. Grabbem had often had the uneasy feeling that if he gave the professor a hearty slap on the back, the professor's face would fall off and reveal what was really underneath. Maybe he had the face of a **man-sized mosquito**. Or maybe metal face bones with blinking lights among them, and a dark grille for a mouth …

"Pull yourself together," he said gruffly to himself. "Business is business and their money's good."

He folded away the laptop and rolled over to go to sleep.

Tomorrow's Big Tour was going to be a triumph. The best one yet. He'd make a fortune.

Just so long as the staff did their jobs, the guests' children all behaved themselves, and most importantly, *nothing out of the ordinary happened*.

If any of the guests got the impression that Grabbem Industries wasn't a well-ordered company where everything ran like clockwork, they might pull out. They had to see machines running smoothly, computers humming softly, elevators going up and down like they were supposed to, and people silently getting on with their jobs as obediently as terrified children in a classroom.

There had been a few too many "incidents" lately. That interfering boy and his stolen Grabbem robot had caused Mr. Grabbem no end of trouble, shutting down operations here and blowing up company property there, until Mr. Grabbem had been so frustrated he'd built a colossal robot of his own to take them down. It hadn't ended well.

"Those two wouldn't come here," he mumbled into his pillow. "They'd never be that bold ..."

Mr. Grabbem was soon snoring like a big happy hog in a bed of straw.

His mind was quiet, dark, as calm as an aquarium with no fish in it. He had no idea what was going to happen the next morning. No idea at all.

If he could have seen what was going to happen twelve hours into the future, he would have jumped out of bed and **run screaming into the night** in his fuzzy pajamas.

Meanwhile, in a room down the hall, his son, Gus Grabbem Junior, was wide awake.

Gus didn't have *friends* the way ordinary children do. Instead, he had a clique of rich-kid cronies who were almost as obnoxious as he was. They didn't have fun together the way that you or I would. Instead, their nastiness merged into a sort of **ghastly clump** like what remains after crayons have been left on a heater.

They called themselves the **Toxic Tweens**. Together they were somehow much worse than any one of them could be on their own. It was a blessing for the rest of the world that they didn't get to meet up more than once a year.

While the parents were off having the Big Tour, Gus and the Toxic Tweens were going to make life horrible for the poor Grabbem employees. There were smoke bombs to throw, **slime canisters** to explode, water cannons to let off, computer systems to fry ... and the best part of all was that the workers

couldn't do anything about it. They had to smile and get on with their jobs or they'd be fired immediately.

"Oh, we're going to have fun, all right." Gus smirked, as he made his plans. "And nothing and nobody is going to stop us!"

CHAPTER 4

The MOT-BOL moved silently through the sky. It was early dawn. Only an hour to go until Axel and BEAST arrived at Platinum Acres.

Axel wished he could just stay up here. He'd never felt less prepared for a mission. He had no idea what was waiting for them in the massive complex below the ground. He cleaned his glasses nervously just to give his fingers something to do.

"I wish we had a **plan**, BEAST," he said. "Agent Omega usually tells us what the plan is, but he can't do that this time."

"HOW DO YOU THINK THEY CAUGHT HIM?" BEAST asked nervously.

"Maybe they've developed a mind scanner," Axel guessed. "Or maybe they hacked into his emails? Omega's good with computers, but he's not the only expert out there."

"SHOULD WE MAKE A PLAN OURSELVES?"

"Good idea. See if the MOT-BOL has a map of the Grabbem base in its memory. Let's try to figure out where they're keeping him."

Twenty minutes later, they had written a plan on the MOT-BOL's onboard computer and printed it out.

TOP SECRET AGENT OMEGA RESCUE PLAN

> To be torn up and swallowed if anyone catches us

Part One: sneak in

The MOT-BOL will land in the hangar
zone.

> This is where Gus Grabbem Junior keeps his
  cool vehicles, so he may be there - avoid at
  all costs! BEAST, go into SHADO form for extra
  sneakiness.

Part Two: elevator

Sneak around to the MAIN ELEVATOR, which
is guarded by a SENTRY ROBOT called
D4V3.

> BEAST says D4V3 is big but very dumb.

Part Three: hack the system

Take the elevator down into the base and
find a computer terminal for BEAST to
hack - should be lots of these. Find out
where they're keeping Agent Omega and
shut down the security cameras.

> DO NOT FORGET THIS, I MEAN IT, BEAST, THIS IS
  SUPER IMPORTANT, OK

Part Four: bust Omega out

Get to Agent Omega's prison cell. BEAST shifts into OGRE form & punches through the wall.

> Which nobody will see because we've shut down the cameras :)

Part Five: escape

Get into an elevator. BEAST can go under the elevator, then use his foot rockets to blast the whole thing up the shaft and out through the roof.

> This part is BEAST's idea though I'm pretty sure he got it out of a certain Roald Dahl book that he's been reading.

Enemies we may meet:

• Guards (lots and lots)

• Sentry robots

• Gun turrets

• The Grabbem family

RADIOACTIVE DINOSAUR WASPS

> BEAST, that is not even a thing

YES IT IS

Axel sighed and folded the plan away.

At least it was a start. But he still felt out of his depth. What if Agent Omega wasn't even in the Grabbem base? He could be anywhere by now.

And despite what BEAST had said, he wasn't sure he trusted the MOT-BOL. The hologram of Omega could have been a computer animation. All this could be a **really clever trap**, and they were walking right into it ...

His phone pinged. Yumi had sent him a message.

Axel. You never came back to the game, so I'm guessing you're on a mission.

*My mother finally decrypted the rest of that message. Your dad is being held by a group called the **NEURON INSTITUTE**. Sorry I can't tell you any more than that.*

Good luck with your mission, whatever it is.

"BEAST, do you know what the Neuron Institute is?" Axel asked, his heart racing.

"NO. ARE WE GOING THERE? HAS THE PLAN CHANGED?"

Axel wanted badly to say "yes." This new information changed everything. They could find his dad now!

And Agent Omega could wait a little longer to be rescued, couldn't he? He'd understand. And BEAST hadn't really wanted to come here in the first place ...

Then BEAST's ears drooped. "ARE WE ABANDONING AGENT OMEGA?"

Axel swallowed hard and made his decision. "No. We're going to get him out, like we promised."

He glanced out of the window again and

saw the gleaming shapes of buildings below them. They'd finally arrived at the Grabbem Base. Nearby lay an immense blue lake. No, not a lake – a swimming pool! Axel's mind boggled at the size of it. You could fit a fleet of warships in a pool that size.

"Better get ready to rumble," he told BEAST.

BEAST's transparent canopy opened and Axel climbed inside. He thumbed a control

and BEAST instantly *shifted*, his robot body rearranging itself into a new form: SHADO. It was slender and panther like, with long claws extending from the arms.

The MOT-BOL hummed down through the air. A hatch opened in the roof of the vehicle hangar below. The MOT-BOL passed through it and the hatch hissed shut.

A jolt went through the craft as it touched down. Axel looked down and saw they had landed on a metal frame. Only a dim orange light, flashing slowly, revealed the scene before them. This must be where the technicians worked. A ladder led down out of sight.

No going back now, Axel thought.

And they **jumped down into the darkness**.

CHAPTER 5

BEAST dropped silently through the dark and landed on all four feet. Yet instead of a **massive crash**, which is what you might expect when a robot drops down several floors, there was only a soft *boomph* and a slight creaking noise.

Axel was impressed. He lifted SHADO's forepaw so he could see it. There were rubbery pads there, like a cat has on its paws.

They must have soaked up all the force of the impact. He squeezed a control and long claws popped out, then back in. Even more cat features!

"Cool. BEAST, scan the area."

"ENGAGING **NIGHT-VISION** MODE."

The huge hangar where they were standing suddenly seemed to light up around them. It was like a supermarket aisle built to a massive scale, with great racks of shelving on either side. But the "shelves" didn't hold boring things like dog food or trash bags. They held the strangest, most alien-looking vehicles Axel had ever seen.

Next to where the MOT-BOL had parked itself, there was an honest-to-goodness **flying saucer**, complete with a transparent dome in the middle. It looked like a relic from an old science fiction movie. Beside that was something like a car safety seat with a gyroscope on the top and the word ANTIGRAV printed above the headrest.

Beyond were even more fantastic, ridiculous vehicles: a trike covered with metal skulls that had a **laser turret** mounted on it, a see-through bubble you could climb inside and boing around in, a surfboard with tiny jet engines at the back, and even someone's attempt to make a flying broomstick.

"MOVEMENT DETECTED," said BEAST. "Hide, *quick!*"

A door opened in the far end of the hall, looking as tiny as a mouse hole in that great expanse of wall. Two figures came in. One shone a flashlight up at the MOT-BOL.

"Check it out, Kelly. It was here all along!"

"I thought you said that craft there had gone missing?" demanded the other figure.

"I suppose it just came back all by its own sweet self, did it?"

"I … I guess it must have done."

"Come on, Tiago. Let's get this maintenance check over with," came the reply. "I hate this place. **Gives me the creeps.** Sometimes I reckon it's **haunted**."

As the two technicians came toward them, Axel nudged SHADO out of their path and deeper into the shadows.

The flashlight beam flashed in their direction.

Axel froze on the spot.

Now that they weren't moving, SHADO's **stealth mode** switched on and they instantly became **invisible**. The flashlight beam shone right through them.

"What is the matter with you?" snapped Kelly.

"Thuh ... thought I saw something," stammered Tiago. "I don't know what it was, but it was ... big."

"You're going crazy! Too much coffee, that's your problem! Keep your mind on the job, or we won't *have* a job."

Axel remembered to breathe. *Keep it together*, he told himself. *You're barely inside, and you've almost been seen already.*

He watched the nervous technicians walk right past them.

Once the technicians had climbed up to the MOT-BOL's landing platform and were looking in the other direction, he whispered, "Let's get moving, BEAST. The route to the elevator's through those doors up ahead."

SHADO went bounding down the length of the darkened hangar, its footfalls as soft as snowflakes.

Just as they were about to slip through the doors, the overhead lights blazed into life. The hangar was suddenly lit up as bright as day.

Axel brought SHADO to a **screeching halt**. For one terrible second they were clearly visible, then they vanished from sight again. Axel hoped nobody had seen them.

Yells and wild laughter rang out. A crowd of boys and girls, none of them older than Axel, came stampeding through the doors.

Fortunately, they weren't looking Axel's way.

Axel felt his heart give a sick thump as he saw who was at the head of the pack. None other than his **archenemy**, Gus Grabbem Junior. But who were these other strange-looking children?

"Toxic Tween Tearaways are IN THE HOUSE!" screamed Gus. "Let's get this party started!"

"Party! Party!" chanted the gang.

Gus spread his arms. "First up today, it's **joyride** time. Pick a vehicle and jump on board, everyone. Let's have some FUN!"

They all sprinted toward their chosen vehicles.

"That broomstick is *mine*," hissed a girl with stringy black hair.

"I'm having the surfboard!" roared a boy with his hair shaved into a crest.

"Bags the bubble!" squawked a red-faced girl with an English accent.

"We'll take the two-seater death trike," said a set of boy-girl twins with ice-blond hair and fringed white leather jackets.

The technicians peered down from their perch. "Now hold on there, you kids," Tiago called out. "Aren't you meant to be with the tour?"

Tour? What tour? Axel thought.

"My dad owns this whole place, you **crusty booger**," screamed Gus, his hands on his hips. "I can go where I like, and so can my guests!"

"Safety rules say you can't," said the technician bravely.

Gus's face broke into a slow grin. "I've got a new idea. Time for some target practice, guys. Let's buzz them!"

Whooping and hollering, the Toxic Tweens fired up their vehicles. In seconds, they turned the hangar into a **roaring nightmare** of noise and smoke.

With Gus leading the way in the antigrav chair, they flew past the terrified technicians, missing them by inches. The technicians clung to the rails of their platform and ducked out of the way as best they could. There was no way to escape. Tiago started down the platform's ladder, but the blond twins went **zooming** past fast enough to knock him clean off it. He changed his mind and just huddled there, whimpering.

"We should have gotten out of here while we had the chance," Axel whispered.

The English girl quickly mastered the art of steering the bouncing bubble. It **boinged** around the room at amazing heights, almost reaching up to the ceiling.

"Look at me!" she crowed. "Watch this, Gus. I'm going to knock those two peasants off and break their silly necks for them. Just see if I don't!"

She came rolling over to get a good run-up.

"Oh no," groaned Axel as the bubble hurtled toward them. "If she hits us, we'll move and turn visible – right in front of Gus Junior!"

CHAPTER 6

"Smash them to bits, Pippa!" yelled the twins.

"Here I go!" bellowed the bubble girl. Her face had turned so red it looked like one big boil. "Three, two, one ..."

The bubble loomed in front of them. Axel had only moments to act. If he moved, everyone would see him. If he didn't, she'd crash into them.

At the last second, he squeezed the claw control.

SHADO's long claws popped out – and into the bubble's taut skin.

There was a terrific **bang** and a horrible shriek.

The red-faced girl lay spread-eagled on the concrete floor, gasping. The remains of the bubble clung tightly to her. She looked like she

had been **shrink-wrapped**.

Axel checked to make sure they were still invisible. They were. ***That was too close.***

The black-haired girl came whooshing down on the rocket

broomstick. "Aww, poor Pippa, what a tragedy." She smirked. "The Sausage Princess went pop!"

"It's not funny, Belladonna!" wailed the girl in the burst bubble. "This thing's stuck to me. I can't move my arms and legs!"

"What happened?" demanded Gus.

Up on the platform, Kelly the technician folded her arms. "You kids broke an expensive piece of equipment, that's what happened. Maybe next time you'll listen!"

Gus narrowed his eyes. "That bubble's made of reinforced Grabstic. It's meant to be unbreakable. What did you do, Pippa?"

Axel didn't move a muscle.

"I didn't do anything, it just popped!" sniveled Pippa. She struggled inside the Grabstic, but couldn't stand up, let alone walk.

Gus snorted in disgust. "I was getting bored anyway. Time to move on, gang." He pointed at Kelly and Tiago. "*You* and *you*, take *her* down to the hospital wing. They can get the Grabstic off her with a laser peeler."

Pippa bawled after him: "Gus, no! Wait for me! I don't want to miss out on all the fun!"

But the Toxic Tweens were already trooping out of the hangar. The fun had already gone out of this game for them. Who their next victim would be, Axel could only guess.

The two technicians climbed down the ladder, loaded Pippa onto a cart and wheeled her out of the room, leaving Axel and BEAST alone.

"That could have been a complete disaster," Axel said. "We've got to be a lot more careful."

"SHOULD WE CHANGE THE PLAN?"

"Yeah. I'm not risking running into Gus and those kids again. Show me the map."

Axel tried to find a way to the main elevator that wouldn't use any of the key corridors. It seemed impossible. All the routes were **heavily guarded**. Then BEAST helpfully highlighted the ventilation system.

"Classic video game strategy," Axel said, approvingly. "Good call. We should probably watch out for big spinning fans and stuff like that, though."

BEAST found a vent cover and popped it open with SHADO's claws. The metal tunnel beyond was only just big enough for him to fit inside. They went **skittering** down into a maze of pipes that twisted and turned, leading them away from the surface and deeper into the underground complex.

They clambered through pipes for what

seemed like hours. When they finally found the hatch leading out through the ceiling of the corridor below, Axel felt relieved. Despite what video games had led him to expect, they hadn't had to jump through any fan blades, leap across chasms filled with toxic waste, or even dodge under thumping hammers.

He said, "Well, at least that part was easy. Maybe *too* easy."

The sound of shouting voices reached their ears. It was Gus Junior and his crowd, without a doubt. Axel and BEAST froze and waited for them to pass by beneath.

When everything was quiet again, Axel lifted the hatch a crack and peeked through.

He stifled a **gasp of fear** as he caught his first glimpse of **D4V3**, the elevator guard robot.

D4V3 stood in front of the doors like a sentry. He looked like a muscle man made from gleaming chrome, but his jutting jaw and helmetlike head made Axel think of the military. One of his arms ended in a **fist**, the other in what looked like a **gun barrel**.

"OH DEAR. THEY HAVE UPGRADED HIM," said BEAST. "HE DID NOT HAVE ALL THAT ARMOR WHEN I SAW HIM LAST."

"Oh, fantastic," Axel said.

"OR THAT **ELECTRO-FIST**."

"Brilliant."

"OR THAT GUN."

Axel face-palmed.

BEAST made the soft pinging noise he made when he was scanning something. "THEY HAVE, HOWEVER, NOT UPGRADED HIS BRAIN," he announced. "IT IS STILL THE SAME **BUDGET MICRO-BRAIN** IT USED TO BE."

Axel stared in disbelief at the words on his screen. According to BEAST's scanners, D4V3, the enormous sentry, had the brain of something much less impressive.

"This guy started out as a *floor scrubber?*"

"YES. HE WAS A ROBOTIC CLEANING UNIT, ABOUT THE SIZE OF A TRASH CAN LID."

"What on earth happened?"

"HE WAS PROMOTED."

Axel struggled to take that information in.

"How ... I mean, why would Grabbem use the brain of a floor scrubber for one of their most heavily armed guard robots?"

"HE WAS A VERY AGGRESSIVE FLOOR SCRUBBER," said BEAST, as if that explained everything.

Axel checked the plan they'd written earlier. "We'd planned to sneak around him, or fight him. I'm not feeling too good about either of those."

"BEAST WILL FIGHT IF HE HAS TO," said BEAST, but Axel could tell he was just trying to be brave again. No way were they going to attack that **armored nightmare** of a sentry robot. Even a **sneak attack** wouldn't get through his armor. There was just no way to get down to the lower levels and free Agent Omega.

Then D4V3 began to mutter to himself as

he watched the hall: "Rotten human kids. Nasty, messy human kids. Running around like they own the place."

"I guess he doesn't like Gus Junior's crew either," Axel said.

Then a thought popped into his head. D4V3 had said *messy*. That gave him an idea.

"Hey. Back when D4V3 was a cleaning robot, what sort of mess made him most angry?"

"CHEWING GUM," responded BEAST immediately. "IT DROVE HIM WILD."

Axel took a stick of chewing gum out of his pocket. "Okay. I think I might have a plan. But if this doesn't work and he catches me, you're going to have to rescue two humans today ..."

CHAPTER 7

At that moment, Mr. Grabbem was leading the members of the Big Tour through the Planning Room. This was a sort of exhibition hall. Little models of landscapes and buildings showed which part of the world Grabbem Industries was going to wreck next.

"Feast your eyes!" he told his guests. "Check out the Rain Forest Ripper. Designed that one myself. Over here we've got the plans for the **Dolphin Slicing Factory**. Young Gus came up with that after we let him play with the kitchen blender ..."

A voice boomed out over the loudspeakers. "*Lady Porkington-Trotter to the hospital wing, please. There has been a minor accident.*"

Lady Porkington-Trotter squealed, "Pippa!" and rushed out of the room.

Startled guests broke into anxious muttering.

"What's that? Accident?"

"Something's wrong!"

"I thought we were *safe* ..."

"Nothing to worry about," said Mr. Grabbem through a clench-toothed grin. "Everything's fine! Just kids messing around." He whispered to his wife: "Shona, get that fool on the speakers to shut their silly mouth, *now*."

"I'm on it," she snapped, and vanished out of the room.

Justin Smoothley's chihuahua let out a series of frightened yips that made Mr. Grabbem want to bake it in a pie.

"Lysander's getting a headache." Justin pouted.

Mrs. Grabbem glided back into the room, as calm as a **vampire** but a lot more suntanned, and whispered in Mr. Grabbem's ear. "It's dealt with. I fired them."

"That's my girl," said Mr. Grabbem, still smiling.

Axel popped the gum into his mouth and started chewing.

"I'll use this to make a mess and distract him, then we'll both run past while he's busy. Okay?"

"OKAY. PLEASE DO NOT GET CAPTURED."

"I'll try not to."

Axel climbed out of BEAST, opened the ceiling grate, waited until D4V3 was looking the other way and then dropped down to the floor. The *slap* of his sneakers on the floor made D4V3 whip his head around and glare.

"Identify yourself!" the robot grated.

Axel thought fast. "I'm Kevin," he said.

"FULL name?"

Axel realized he should have thought up a fake name before doing this, but it was too late.

"Kevin ... Snot," he said, hoping he sounded convincing. "I'm with the tour."

D4V3 wasn't buying it. "Kevin Snot? Don't have that name on record. Which company are you from?"

"None of your business!" Axel said. Having to be rude made him feel terrible, especially since the robot was only doing his job, but there were more important things at stake.

He took the gum out of his mouth and dropped it on the floor, right where D4V3 could see it.

Deep inside D4V3's tiny robot brain, a long-forgotten circuit suddenly went into overdrive.

"PICK THAT UP!" he boomed.

Axel trod on the gum and ground it into the floor with his heel. "Nah," he said. He sauntered away.

D4V3 began to vibrate all over, like a washing machine going into its spin cycle. Little jets of steam hissed out of his head as his system began to overheat. He was **mad**.

"KEVIN SNOT, I ORDER YOU TO CLEAN UP THIS MESS IMMEDIATELY!"

"Clean it up yourself," Axel sneered. "What's the matter? Don't you know how?" He let out a laugh that he hoped sounded suitably evil.

BEAST watched him through the ceiling hatch, his eyes wide.

Long ago, when D4V3 had been a floor-scrubbing robot, he had worked hard to get rid of the mess the humans left behind all day long. Regular dirt was bad. Spilled food was worse. But chewing gum was the **worst mess** of all. It was **sticky** and **stretchy** and clogged up his bristles.

Now, as he stared at the disgusting gray blob of gum on the perfectly clean floor, all those angry memories came boiling up again. He had to get rid of it right now.

"Gum!" he roared. "Horrible gum! Clean it up, clean it up!"

While D4V3 bellowed and raved with his back turned, Axel looked up and quickly mouthed, "*Now!*"

BEAST nodded. He leapt down in SHADO form.

Axel thumbed the elevator button and hoped the doors would open quickly.

But something was wrong. D4V3 looked at the arm with the fist. He looked at the arm with the gun barrel. He looked down at his feet. "Arrrgh," he moaned. "I need my brushes. I can't find where my brushes have gone!"

"Oh no. That's bad," Axel whispered.

D4V3's eyes blazed crimson. Steam blasted out of his head like a foggy halo. He pointed his gun-barrel arm down at the blob of gum. "WHO NEEDS BRUSHES ANYWAY?" he screamed. "I HAVE SOMETHING BETTER

RIGHT HERE! IT'S CLEAN-UP TIME, GUMMO!"

Axel and BEAST dived for cover.

The next second, in a blinding, deafening barrage of sound and light, the full force of D4V3's **plasma cannon** opened up on one small piece of gum.

The weapon had been designed to **blow holes through tanks** and **knock satellites out of orbit**. It had not been intended to be used for indoor cleaning jobs. As a result, several **disastrous** things happened, one after the other.

The first disaster was that the plasma cannon removed not only the gum, but the floor that surrounded it in a fifteen-foot radius.

That alone would have been bad enough. But the plasma beam didn't stop there. It kept going, reducing a vending machine to atoms on the way, and punched right through the *next* floor. Then it burst through the floor after that, and the floor after that, until it had scorched a hole through *forty-one floors*. Imagine you have a cake with forty-one layers, and then someone who really hates cake shoots a single arrow through the entire cake in one shot.

The *second* disaster was that D4V3, having shot away the floor directly beneath his own feet, immediately fell down the hole. Axel heard his robotic wail grow steadily fainter until it stopped with a sudden crash.

The *third* disaster was that the alarms went off. Because a robot blowing a hole through your building is not going to go unnoticed.

Axel stared down into the smoldering pit in front of them. Glowing, molten girders jutted out of its sides. Everything had gone very wrong very fast.

BEAST's ears twitched. "AXEL, WE ARE IN **GREAT DANGER**. THERE ARE GUARDS COMING!"

"From which direction?"

"FROM EVERYWHERE!"

Now Axel could hear it too – the sound of boots pounding and orders being shouted.

The elevator was almost here. But would it be a way out, or would it be full of guards? He couldn't take the chance.

He hoisted himself back up into BEAST's chest cavity. "We can't fight that many. We've got to get out of here."

"BUT THERE IS NOWHERE TO RUN TO!" wailed BEAST.

Axel looked around, then down at the gaping hole. "Oh, yes, there is. We go *down*.

Get into PILLBUG form!"

BEAST *shifted*. Metal screens fanned out across his body, enclosing him in a ball of thick armor. Only his eyes could be seen, looking out of a little gap.

Axel rolled him up into a ball. He couldn't see anything at all now.

Time for a leap into the dark. He took a deep breath and rolled BEAST over the edge.

CHAPTER 8

Meanwhile, Mr. Grabbem was showing his guests around the Experiment Lab. This was his favorite part of the tour.

"In this room we're developing an acid so powerful it can eat through anything!" he said.

Professor Payne frowned. "Really? Then what are you going to keep it in?"

Mr. Grabbem's grin faltered, then came back twice as strong. "Ha-ha-ha! Good one. I'm sure we'll figure something out. Now, in this next room, we're working on a method to turn whales directly into oil. Every bit of them, bone, brain and all. Imagine that!"

"Very good idea," said General Regan. "Nothing more useless than a whale. Just great mounds of blubber taking up space in our oceans."

At that point, the alarms went off.

Mr. Grabbem turned a shocking shade of pink. He hissed in his wife's ear, "NOW what's the matter?"

She checked her tablet. "**Robot malfunction** by the main elevator," she whispered back. "Fire on multiple floors ... serious damage ... a whole row of machines destroyed ..."

Mr. Grabbem growled, "On my big day? What a coincidence. Someone's trying to ruin the tour."

"What do we do?"

"Send a message to Robotics. I want the **Crusherbots** armed and ready."

"Is there a *fire?*" gasped Justin Smoothley.

"DRILL!" shrieked Mr. Grabbem in a voice so loud it made Lysander the chihuahua wet himself.

Mr. Grabbem leaned, panting hard, against the wall. "Just a fire drill," he said. "Nothing to worry about." His shirt was sweaty under his arms.

Professor Payne gave him a cool, calculating look. "Are you being completely honest with us, Grabbem?"

Mr. Grabbem made an offended face. "My *dear* professor. Would I lie?"

Inside BEAST, Axel was flung every which way at once as they fell through floor after floor, plummeting down the length of the plasma-blasted shaft. Any second now they'd come to a **crashing halt**. He could only hope BEAST's armor was strong enough to survive the fall.

But when they finally hit the ground, it wasn't with a crash.

It wasn't even with a bang.

It was more of a *plop*.

Axel waited for his world to stop spinning. "BEAST, what happened? Are you okay?"

"NO DAMAGE," BEAST said. "YET."

"What do you mean, 'yet'?" Axel fanned his face. It was hot all of a sudden.

"PILLBUG FORM IS NOT FIREPROOF.

WE HAVE LANDED IN **MOLTEN METAL**."

"*What?*"

But as soon as he'd said it, Axel figured it out. D4V3's plasma beam must have blazed right into whatever Grabbem machinery was on this level and melted it. PILLBUG had splashed down into white-hot **liquid metal**!

"THE METAL IS ALREADY COOLING DOWN," said BEAST. "THAT IS THE GOOD PART. THE BAD PART IS THAT IF IT COOLS DOWN ANY FURTHER WE WILL BE TRAPPED."

Axel had a vision of BEAST encased forever in a lump of steel, with him as a little skeleton body inside, and almost freaked out on the spot.

"Can you still shift?"

"I THINK SO."

"Go into MYTHFIRE form, quick!"

BEAST **shifted**. The armor plates of PILLBUG slid away, and for a horrible moment all of BEAST's heat sensors turned a screaming red. Axel shielded his eyes from the blinding glare of the liquid metal. He could smell burning.

The next moment, BEAST's arms became clawed limbs and his head became reptilian. His dragon form, MYTHFIRE, took over. The heat sensors stabilized; MYTHFIRE was immune to heat.

Axel flung out MYTHFIRE's claw, caught hold of the edge and hauled them up from the scalding pit.

MYTHFIRE clambered out of the silvery, smoking liquid as if it had been a hot bath. Puddles of metal as bright as mercury lay in his wake.

Axel took a look around, trying to get his bearings.

They had fallen a *long* way underground. D4V3's plasma cannon had blasted through into the Factory Levels. They were in a great, gloomy hall where robotic arms assembled Grabbem machines on conveyor belts, lighting up the darkness with blue crackling sparks. The floor was solid steel, except for the part that the plasma beam had turned into a molten jacuzzi.

Axel turned MYTHFIRE's armor up to full blast, to melt away any scraps of steel that were still clinging to them.

"Are you okay?"

"ONLY MINOR DAMAGE."

"Well, we made it into the base, nobody knows we're here, and we're still alive," Axel said. "So far, so good, I guess. Remind me what we're meant to do next?"

"FIND A COMPUTER TERMINAL."

"Great. That could take hours! What do they look like?"

"LIKE THAT," said BEAST, and pointed at the little gray computer terminal that was running the factory machines.

"Oh," said Axel.

Our luck's changed, he thought. But he didn't say it out loud, in case that jinxed it.

BEAST plugged his finger into the side of

the terminal. The screen filled up with random gobbledygook. Columns and columns of letters and numbers shot past with blinding speed.

"ACCESSING FILES," said BEAST. "SEARCHING ..."

"We're looking for Cedric Bunk," said Axel. "That's Agent Omega's real name. He didn't want to tell us, but Mom point-blank refused to write 'Agent Omega' on his birthday card."

"SEARCHING ..." said BEAST.

Axel decided to keep quiet. There was nothing he could do to help. It was all on BEAST now.

"LOCATED!"

"You've found him? Where?"

"OPERATIVE BUNK IS IN THE HOSPITAL WING, ISOLATION WARD."

Axel gasped. "The hospital, not the prison?

That means he's hurt. We've got to get to him right away."

Anger swept through him, washing away all traces of fear. What could have happened? Had Agent Omega tried to fight Grabbem when they found out he was a double agent? Could they have **poisoned** him, even? It didn't matter. He was going to get his friend out of there, even if he had to carry his unconscious body out in his arms.

"Unplug yourself, BEAST. We're leaving."

BEAST hesitated. "I AM SURE THERE WAS SOMETHING ELSE I WAS MEANT TO DO."

"Forget it. There isn't time. We're going to the hospital, *now!*"

Up on the wall, a security camera turned to watch them.

CHAPTER 9

The good news was that the hospital wing wasn't far away. They could be there in five minutes. The bad news was that the route they needed to take was a really busy one. It led past the cafeteria and the bathrooms, so lots of Grabbem staff would be constantly coming and going.

"We're so close!" Axel said. "How are we going to do this? It's not like we can just walk through the base and pretend to be Grabbem employees."

BEAST pointed to some coveralls hanging by one of the machines. "YOU COULD WEAR THOSE."

"Yeah, but what about you? They don't make coveralls in your size," Axel said drily.

"MAYBE BEAST SHOULD JUST WAIT HERE, THEN," said BEAST.

He sounded gloomy. Axel knew that was a warning sign.

Sometimes, despite all the amazing things he could do, BEAST started to doubt himself and feel like he was a burden. At times like those, Axel had to make sure BEAST knew how important he was. If BEAST got into a slump now, he might want to **turn into a fridge** and do nothing at all, and then they'd be stuck ...

A fridge. Of course.

Just like that, Axel had the answer. He took a USB drive out of his pocket.

Hundreds of people milled around outside the cafeteria, talking, drinking and complaining about work.

Not one of them gave Axel a second look as he walked past, pushing a cart along. He was wearing the coveralls they'd found, with a cap pulled down low to hide his face.

On the cart lay a very high-tech-looking fridge with smart black and green panels. There were two spots that looked a little like closed eyes on the front.

When they reached the security checkpoint halfway down the hall, the guard on duty looked at them wearily. "Where you taking that?"

"New fridge for the break room," Axel mumbled.

"Glory be. They're finally sending us something useful. Go on, in you go."

A green light went on and the door slid open. Heart thumping, Axel wheeled the fridge through. It hummed softly to itself as it passed by.

Never gonna give you up, thought the guard. *Never gonna let you down ... wait, why am I thinking of that song?*

But the fridge had already gone.

Axel strode on with his head down. He was no longer sure whether he was excited, terrified, or a bit of both. He was right in the heart of the enemy's operations, and they didn't even know. After all they'd been through, he was going to rescue his friend right under Mr. Grabbem's nose!

"Watch where you're going!" snapped a horribly familiar voice.

Axel saw he'd nearly run the cart wheel over two shiny black shoes. He glanced up – and nearly fainted from **pure fright**. He really WAS under Mr. Grabbem's nose. The real Mr. Grabbem was right here, right next to him!

"Sorry, sir," he mumbled. "My fault, sir. Won't happen again, sir."

To his amazement, Mr. Grabbem patted his shoulder with a sweaty hand.

"No worries. Keep working, lad." He turned to his companions. "See, here's a worker who knows his place. Humble, you see? They don't get above themselves here at Grabbem Industries!"

Axel sneaked a look at the group of people Mr. Grabbem was talking to. What

a **ghastly** crowd. They all had the same **mean look** in their eyes, and the same arrogant attitude as Grabbem.

"Weaselly little whelp," snarled a woman in a military jacket.

A handsome blond man stroked his chihuahua and sneered. "I think you're being too generous, Grabbem, employing *his* sort."

"If that had been one of *my* workers, I'd have planted an **obedience chip** in his brain," said a tall, bald, very pale man.

Mr. Grabbem chuckled and wagged a finger. "That might be how you do things at the Neuron Institute, Professor Payne, but around here we're not in the Frankenstein business!"

They all laughed, except for the professor, who just stared blankly.

Axel's legs suddenly didn't want to work.

Keep walking, he told himself.

But he could hardly stand upright. The words echoed in his mind. Mr. Grabbem had said **Neuron Institute**. The pale, bald man was from the very same place where Axel's father was being held prisoner! A place so mysterious that even Yumi's family knew next to nothing about it.

Now he had a chance. If he could follow them, listen to their conversations, he might learn where the **Neuron Institute** was based. **Where his father was.**

Or he could tell BEAST to grab the professor and *make* the man tell him what he needed to know.

The tour group started to move away down the hall.

Axel kept walking. He wanted to scream.

I have to keep going and rescue Agent Omega. He needs me. But my father needs me, too! And if I don't take this chance, it won't come again!

He had to turn around. It was now or never.

What am I going to do?

His heart breaking, Axel made his decision ...

CHAPTER 10

Nobody spared Axel a glance as he pushed BEAST, still in FRIJ form, through the swinging doors of the hospital wing. He was glad of that. There were tears in his eyes.

I'm sorry, Dad, he thought. *But Yumi was right when she said I always had to stick to the mission goal, instead of rushing off on wild-goose chases. Right now, I need to focus on rescuing Agent Omega. He's counting on me. But I promise when he's safely out of here, I'll find a way to come and save you, too.*

They passed hospital beds as they went. Pippa the Sausage Princess lay in one of them, howling as a doctor pulled the sticky Grabstic off her in long strips. He could still hear her yells as he pushed BEAST into the elevator at the end of the room.

They rode down to the isolation ward. A little camera in the elevator watched them.

The isolation ward turned out to be a row of glass-walled cells. It wasn't a prison, but it was pretty close to one. Axel was glad to see there were no doctors or nurses here at all. Most of the cells were empty, but Axel caught sight of a familiar figure in the last cell on the right, sitting up in bed.

"There he is! Agent Omega! It's me, Axel!"

He ran for the cell. BEAST, still in FRIJ form, tried to totter after him, fell over and went **clang**. "SHIFTING," BEAST said, sounding embarrassed. He turned back into his regular form.

Agent Omega jumped out of bed. His face was covered with **bright-blue dots**. "Oh, Axel. Oh, you poor brave boy. You came for me. I was hoping you wouldn't, but you did. Of course you did."

Axel's mouth fell open. "You were hoping I *wouldn't?*"

Agent Omega looked like the most miserable man on Earth. "I'm a fool. The MOT-BOL was set up to go and fetch you if I ever didn't put the password in. Because I thought the only possible reason that could happen would be if they'd caught me."

For a moment, Axel fought against the truth. It was **hammering its fists on his brain**, but he didn't want to let it in. Because if he did, it would mean that all of this had been for nothing.

But he knew he had no choice. The spots on Agent Omega's face, the secure medical room ... they all added up to one conclusion.

"They hadn't caught you at all!" Axel realized. "They were just keeping you locked up in here because you've got some kind of horrible illness. That's why you couldn't put your password in!"

"Pixel pox," said Agent Omega gloomily. "It's highly contagious. They had to keep me away from the other employees."

Axel sank against the glass wall. He didn't know whether to laugh or cry. "Do you have any idea what we went through to get here?"

"Listen," Omega said. "The robo-doctor will be back any second. I need to tell you that *this wasn't a waste of time.*"

"Well, it sure feels like one!" Axel wiped his nose.

"No! Today is the Grabbems' Big Tour. They're taking a bunch of mega-rich people around the base, trying to impress them. And what have they seen? **Chaos.** I heard all the announcements on the loudspeakers." Omega counted off on his fingers: "Guests hospitalized. **Robots blowing holes through the floor.** Fire alarms going off.

Machinery wrecked. His computer system broken into. You think any of them are going to give him money now?"

"So that's who those people were," Axel said.

"You've hit Grabbem where he'll feel it most. In his pocket!"

"MOTION DETECTED," said BEAST. "IT IS THE ROBO-DOCTOR."

"Stall him," said Axel.

"HOW?"

"I don't know. Make something up!"

BEAST went stomping off around the corner while Axel told Agent Omega all about Yumi's message and the professor. When he heard the words "Neuron Institute," Omega's eyes brightened.

"Axel, I know who they are," he said. "Better still, I know *where* they are. I've been researching them ever since I saw that the professor was one of Grabbem's investors."

"You mean we can go get my dad?" Axel yelled.

"Yes! All the files are on my computer! The moment this Pixel Pox clears up, I'll send you everything you need to know. But for now, you have to get out of here. Go home!"

Axel didn't need telling twice. He ran back down the hall and found BEAST talking to a

slender silver figure with a lamp on its head. That must be the robot doctor.

"And when did you first notice the symptoms of this ... what did you call it ... **'punching sickness'**?" the robot doctor asked.

"RIGHT NOW," said BEAST, and punched the robot doctor in the face.

"Run!" yelled Axel.

They ran.

They reached the elevator, but the doors were closed and the display said the elevator was on a floor below. Axel pressed the button. The elevator began to rise. Very slowly.

"We haven't got time for this. BEAST, pull the doors open."

BEAST hauled back the doors, bending and buckling them. Axel looked up the empty elevator shaft. Nothing in their way. Good.

He climbed inside BEAST and shifted him into SKYHAWK form.

"Always wondered what would happen if I tried to fly SKYHAWK indoors," he said. "Here goes ..."

SKYHAWK flew forward into the shaft and banked sharply up. Axel increased the power. They went flying up the smooth walls of the shaft like a bullet from a rifle barrel. Sparks raced from SKYHAWK's wing tips as they brushed the metal.

Axel could still make out the shaft's end wall, **rushing toward them faster than an oncoming train**.

In seconds they would run out of shaft. There was no room to turn, and no time to slow down.

Axel shifted the thrusters to MAXIMUM, and waited.

Meanwhile, Mr. Grabbem was escorting his guests toward the grand finale of the Big Tour. "Hurry to the Testing Zone, folks! We can't be late! Tell the kiddies to meet us there."

"Is there some reason why we're going to the Testing Zone early?" demanded Professor Payne.

"Oh, yes. Trust me, it'll be worth it."

Mrs. Grabbem listened to someone talking on her phone, nodded and gave her husband a cold grin. "Just got a sighting on level twenty-three. The boy and his robot are on the way. They don't suspect a thing."

CHAPTER 11

Axel piled on more power and they climbed faster and faster. The shaft was a blur now, going by too fast to see.

"BEAST, go into PILLBUG form, *now!*"

With less than a second to spare, BEAST shifted into his most armored form and balled up.

They didn't have SKYHAWK's engines to propel them anymore, but BEAST was already going faster than a rocket. They **smashed** through the end of the shaft like a **cannonball** and kept going. They **punched** through the concrete floor and erupted out the other side in a shower of masonry dust.

When they had rolled to a stop, Axel cautiously unfolded PILLBUG.

"I wasn't sure that was going to work. BEAST, where are we?"

"WE ARE NEAR THE MAIN ENTRANCE, IN THE TESTING ZONE."

Axel had expected to come up in an open-air parking lot. Instead, they had burst through the floor of some sort of arena with rows of seats around it. There were **pillars with spikes on them**, nozzles that jetted fire every few seconds, and treacherous-looking poles leading out over open pits.

"What are they testing here? On second thought, I don't want to know. Let's go."

There was a metal roller door at the end that must be the exit. Beyond lay freedom. Axel started for it, but a voice rang out over the loudspeakers:

"Not leaving so soon, I hope?"

It was Mr. Grabbem.

Above the rows of seats was a royal box. Axel looked on in horror as the Grabbem family sat down in it, along with their guests and the Toxic Tweens.

"THIS IS BAD," said BEAST.

"I think it's worse than bad," stammered Axel.

"Ladies and gentlemen!" bellowed Mr. Grabbem. "Here before you is a certain annoying little brat who has been doing his level best to ruin this very special day."

"Boo!" screamed the Toxic Tweens.

"Shame!" yelled Lady Porkington-Trotter.

"Varmint!" thundered Hengist Punkerdunk.

Mr. Grabbem gloated like a Roman emperor who was about to have a gladiator fight a pack of angry leopards – armed only with a spoon.

"Did you think we wouldn't spot you, boy? Don't you know there are cameras all over this place?"

Axel groaned. "We forgot to turn the cameras off when we hacked the terminal!"

"I **KNEW** THERE WAS SOMETHING I WAS SUPPOSED TO DO," sighed BEAST.

"Since the little twerp has popped up in our Testing Zone," crowed Mr. Grabbem, "I'd like to do some testing. Testing to destruction!"

All the Toxic Tweens laughed and jeered. Mrs. Grabbem stepped forward with an elegant swish.

"I'd like to take this opportunity to show off one of our latest Grabbem creations, **the remote-control Crusherbot**, ideal for demolishing other people's homes from a safe distance."

"Nice sales pitch," grunted General Regan.

"We'd like you all to join in with this

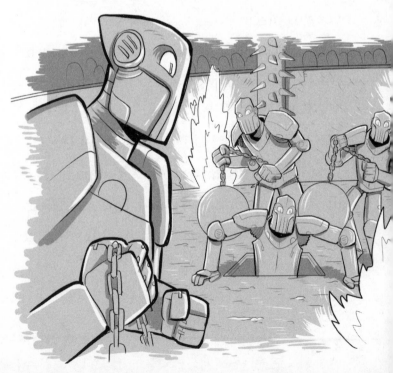

demonstration. Reach under your chairs and you'll find a controller each," Mrs. Grabbem said. "Now bring on the Crusherbots!"

Square holes slid open in the ground. Ten-foot robots came clambering up from them, each one carrying a round ball on the end of a chain.

They looked like **a cross between medieval knights and demolition cranes**.

"**You** get a Crusherbot," said Mrs. Grabbem, "and **you**, and **you! Crusherbots for everyone!**"

With squeals of glee, the Grabbems and their tour guests operated their controllers. The Crusherbots moved, obeying their commands. They marched stiffly toward BEAST, swinging their demolition balls menacingly.

"This is fun," giggled Justin Smoothley. "Come on, Lysander, help me press the bitty button. Squash his silly head!"

Axel and BEAST had been outnumbered before, but never like this. Axel couldn't even count how many Crusherbots were coming at them. Ten? Twelve? How could they possibly fight that many?

"AXEL, I THINK THIS IS THE END," said BEAST.

"No!" Axel yelled. "We *have* to get out of here. **I have to save my dad!**"

He fired BEAST's foot thrusters and flew for the exit.

"No, you don't," shouted Gus Grabbem Junior. He flung his Crusherbot's demolition ball. It whizzed up, trailing its chain, and wrapped around BEAST's leg. The Crusherbot yanked hard, and BEAST came crashing down.

Gus Junior's Crusherbot hauled the ball back and swung it around in a whizzing figure eight. "I'd finish you off now," Gus said, "but Dad says I need to let my friends have a turn beating you up first!"

"I AM SORRY," BEAST said, sounding broken. "I WAS NOT STRONG ENOUGH."

"Shift to OGRE," Axel said. "We'll show them who's strong."

The nearest Crusherbots, controlled by Lady Porkington-Trotter and Hengist Punkerdunk, went on the attack. They clumsily swung their wrecking balls at BEAST, but they weren't gamers like Axel was, and they weren't used to using controllers. Axel dodged them easily, grabbed one Crusherbot by the leg and threw it at the other. There was a **horrific crash**, and both the bots went down in a mangled pile of metal.

"Not fair!" Lady Porkington-Trotter howled. She threw her controller away and went off to sulk.

"Leave this to me," snapped General Regan. "Can't expect a civilian like you to understand a war machine like this." Her eyes narrowed as she lined up her attack with military precision.

Axel saw it coming, but he was too late.

The wrecking ball slammed into OGRE's body and knocked him backward off his feet.

General Regan grinned and went in for the kill.

But as she swung at him, Axel caught hold of her wrecking ball's chain and pulled with all of OGRE's strength. Taken by surprise, her Crusherbot fell over and skidded to a halt in the sand. Axel made OGRE jump up in the air and come down with both feet on the fallen Crusherbot's head. It lay still, jetting sparks into the sandy floor.

"One at a time," he panted. "That's how we do this. Take them down one at a time."

Belladonna sent her Crusherbot in next. Her fighting style was much more sneaky. She aimed fake blows at OGRE's head, arms and legs, only to whip them away at the last moment. Axel could hardly keep up.

"Are you going to hit me or not?" he yelled.

"When I feel like it." She smirked.

Axel saw she wasn't looking at him, but at the pillar behind him. It was one of the flame-jet ones. So that was her game – force him to retreat and let the **fiery blast** take him down by surprise! Well, two could play at that game.

He let her push him back and back until he was almost up against the pillar. Then, when he knew the fire jet was coming, he ducked. Belladonna shrieked as the blast melted her Crusherbot's head like a chocolate bunny on a heater.

Professor Payne shook his head in disgust and put his controller down. "I refuse to play. This was an unwise game, Grabbem. I am not impressed. The boy is making you look like an amateur."

"Stop playing around and *rush him!*" yelled Mr. Grabbem.

The guests weren't having fun anymore. This was serious. They worked their controllers and the remaining Crusherbots closed ranks. They formed a circle around OGRE.

Axel desperately looked for a way out. There wasn't one. He couldn't defend against all of them at once.

"I WANT TO SHIFT INTO MYTHFIRE," BEAST said quietly.

"Why?"

"BECAUSE IF THIS IS REALLY THE END, I WANT TO GO OUT IN A BLAZE OF GLORY."

"Do it," Axel said, his voice cracking.

Then, in the distance, Axel heard an engine revving. The sound grew louder and louder.

Gus Grabbem Junior said, "What on earth ..."

In a glorious blast of light, **the metal doors blew apart**.

There, on the other side, was the death trike the twins had piloted earlier that day. Sitting at the laser turret and at the handlebars were Kelly and Tiago, the two technicians from the hangar.

"Hey, kid!" Tiago shouted. "Remember us?"

"You guys? I thought you couldn't see me!" Axel said.

"We've been watching you on the security cameras! Was it you who burst that kid's bubble?"

"Yes!"

"Knew it. We don't know who you are, but **you have guts**. We couldn't leave you with no backup, not after you saved us from those rotten kids," said Tiago.

"Oh, and Mr. Grabbem?" called Kelly. "I've got a message for you. **Grabbem Industries stinks.** I QUIT!"

"Me too!" said Tiago.

Pure chaos broke out then. General Regan pointed and yelled at the top of her voice. Mrs. Grabbem turned pale under her fake tan. Mr. Grabbem just stood and stared without blinking, as if his brain had fallen out.

Not one of them was paying attention to the robots they were meant to be controlling.

"Now's our chance, BEAST. Go, go, go!"

Axel lowered MYTHFIRE's head and charged. He slammed through the Crusherbots

like a rugby forward and kept going.

Tiago cheered him on. "Run, kid! We've got your back!"

Kelly backed him up with a fresh scatter blast of laser fire. Brilliant bolts **zinged** around the arena, ricocheting off the walls and ceiling. The Grabbem party dived for cover.

Only Gus Junior stayed standing. This game wasn't over yet. He sent his Crusherbot charging after BEAST. But Axel lashed out with MYTHFIRE's tail and knocked the robot flying.

"You hit me from behind once before, remember?" Axel said. "The first time we ever fought. Think I'd let you get away with it again?"

While Gus screamed and yelled about how it "wasn't fair," Axel dived out through the wrecked metal door and shifted BEAST into SKYHAWK.

"You think Kelly and Tiago are going to be okay?" he asked.

"I THINK THEY WILL BE IN A LOT OF TROUBLE," said BEAST, "BUT I DO NOT THINK THEY WILL CARE."

Good luck, guys, Axel thought. He hit the thrusters, and SKYHAWK went soaring away. Platinum Acres retreated into the distance like a bad memory.

Axel clung to the controls, breathing hard. He didn't even want to think about slowing down until they were many, many miles away from the Grabbem mansion.

Three nights later, Axel, his mom, Nedra, and their friend Rusty Rosie sat talking to Agent Omega on Skype. He was back in his secret closet, down in the depths of the Grabbem base. His calm face showed no trace of Pixel Pox.

"For a mission that shouldn't have happened in the first place, that was a **major success**," he said.

"I still can't believe you went!" Nedra said.

"I can't believe they didn't take me," Rosie pouted. "My boot has an appointment with Mr. Grabbem's backside. And I'd like to have some words with that slimy wife of his, too."

"I know everyone wants a piece of the action, but Axel and BEAST work best together," said Omega. "Just look at what they managed to do this time. None of the tour guests are investing another penny. **Grabbem's lost a fortune.** His business partners are pulling out of deals. He's even had to sell a whole bunch of his land so he can afford to repair his factories! I never thought I'd say this, but you've got them on the run."

BEAST leaned in. "WHAT HAPPENED TO KELLY AND TIAGO? THAT WAS VERY BRAVE OF THEM."

Agent Omega let out a deep, strong laugh. Axel had never heard him laugh before. "Those guys are the talk of the base!"

"I bet," Axel said.

"Seems just about everyone who works at Grabbem has been storing up a whole lot of anger about the way the boss runs things, and Kelly and Tiago showed them they didn't have to just sit there and take it. Oh, Kelly and Tiago will be just fine. You know why?"

"WHY?"

"Because when they drove off that Grabbem base in their stolen trike, *not a single Grabbem employee saw which way they went*. Isn't that incredible?"

"But there were Grabbem staff all over the

place!" Axel said. "One of them must have seen."

"That's what the boss said, too. 'One of you must have seen!' But nobody did, no matter how angry he got. Crazy, huh?" There was a twinkle in Agent Omega's eye.

"Crazy." Axel grinned.

Agent Omega glanced over his shoulder. "Time for me to go. Grabbem might not have caught me this time, but I can't let my guard down. I'll be in touch soon. We've got a very important mission to plan."

"The Neuron Institute," said Nedra.

Omega nodded. "I know what's riding on this one. I won't let you down. Believe it. Omega out."

The screen went dark. Nobody said anything for a while.

"I AM GLAD KELLY AND TIAGO

MADE IT," said BEAST eventually. "THEY WERE VERY BRAVE."

Axel leaned back in his chair and thought for a while.

"You know, BEAST, I think people are wrong about bravery. People act like it's something you have to pull out of nowhere, all by yourself. But sometimes you can catch it from other people."

"LIKE PIXEL POX?"

Axel laughed. "Exactly! If someone else is brave, it makes it easier for you to be. Bravery is ... what's the word? Contagious."

"THEN BEAST WILL BE AS BRAVE AS HE CAN, ALL THE TIME. AND MAYBE LOTS OF PEOPLE WILL CATCH BRAVERY FROM HIM."

Axel rested his head on BEAST's controls

lovingly, and closed his eyes. *You're already off to a good start,* he thought.

THE END
(for now)

ABOUT THE AUTHOR
& ILLUSTRATOR

ADRIAN C. BOTT is a gamer, writer and professional adventure creator. He lives in Sussex, England, with his family and is allowed to play video games whenever he wants.

ANDY ISAAC lives in Melbourne, Australia. He discovered his love of illustration through comic books when he was eight years old, and has been creating his own characters ever since.

CHAPTER 1

Axel Brayburn couldn't sleep.

He knew he needed rest. Tomorrow he was going on the most important mission of his life. But thinking about that mission was keeping him awake.

Over a year ago, his father, Matt, had gone to pick up some takeout for dinner and had never come home. The police had found his empty car upside down by the side of the road, without a scratch on it. None of the searches had ever turned up a single hair. Months had gone by without any news, but Axel and his mom, Nedra, had never given up hope. His dad had to be alive, somewhere.

Now Axel knew they had been right all along. His dad *was* alive – and being held prisoner by a mysterious, sinister group called the Neuron Institute. Axel had briefly met their leader, a pale man called Professor Payne who had all the charm and personality of a praying mantis.

Axel's alarm clock was a round plastic moon that lit up from within. Glowing green numbers showed the time was a minute before midnight.

Tomorrow, Axel and his shape-shifting robot friend, BEAST, would try to rescue his dad. It sounded simple when you put it like that. But Axel still didn't know what sort of enemies he was going up against, and he wouldn't know until Agent Omega arrived in the morning with the mission briefing.

He tossed and turned in the dark.

Not knowing what he was heading into was worse than knowing, somehow. His sleepy brain kept conjuring up all sorts of horrors. Professor Payne was a scientist. Maybe he made **monsters**. Perhaps there really would be **radioactive dinosaur wasps** this time. Or **shark-spider** hybrids, scuttling across the walls with mouths full of razor teeth. Maybe they would fail, and his father would never come home …

Axel rolled over and groaned into his pillow. This was like Christmas, except instead of presents, the morning would bring a surprise package full of **deadly danger**.

"AXEL?" whispered BEAST from across the room. "ARE YOU OKAY?"

"Can't sleep," Axel mumbled.

"CAN I HELP?"

"Don't know."

"SHOULD I TRY DOING THE OCEAN THING?"

"Sure. May as well."

So BEAST tried his best to sound like the sea, because that always calmed Axel down. He made the **whooshing** sounds of waves **crashing** on the shore and sometimes added the sounds of seabirds. He was careful not to do the lonely cry of a humpback whale because the one time he'd done that, it had come out louder than a car alarm and he'd woken up the entire street by mistake.

It worked. Soon Axel was snoring gently.

BEAST watched him while he slept, just in case.

The next day dawned gray and cold.

Once, Axel's secret den under the house had felt like a private fun room, somewhere to go and relax or play games with BEAST. But now, with everyone gathered around with serious faces and the most important mission of his life ahead of him, it felt more like an army command center.

Agent Omega had arrived before Axel was up. He sat on the sofa, cradling a huge mug of coffee. Beside him sat Rusty Rosie, their loyal friend, and Axel's mom. BEAST stood off to one side. He looked worried, but then, he often did.

"You ready, Axel?" Agent Omega said softly.

Axel nodded.

"Okay. We all know why we're here. This mission has only one goal. Rescue Matt Brayburn from the Neuron Institute and bring him home. Luckily, Axel and BEAST have some experience in rescuing people from **dangerous** places." Omega smiled slightly.

The Omega Operation, Axel thought. *He means the time BEAST and I tried to break him out of the Grabbem base. We barely escaped with our lives!*

"So the same steps as last time?" he asked.

"You got it. Get in, find a terminal, hack it, find out where your dad's being kept. Think of last time as a dry run."

"BEAST KNEW HIS WAY AROUND LAST TIME," said BEAST, twitching his antennae nervously.

"Good point," said Nedra. "We'd all heard of Grabbem Industries, but not these new guys.

What even *is* the Neuron Institute?"

"First, let's look at *where* they are." Omega took a device like a TV remote control from his pocket, pointed it at the table and pressed a button. A 3-D image appeared in the air before them, showing a castle perched high on a bleak mountain.

"Seriously?" Rosie said. "With a name like that I thought they'd be in some fancy science lab, not **Dracula's Castle**."

"Look closer," said Omega, and zoomed the view in. They all saw that the gloomy castle was covered with strange devices. Cables threaded up and down the walls. There were huge screens hanging over the courtyards and satellite-dish-like devices on the tower tops. The windows glowed purple and orange, and vents jetted clouds of steam out into the cold mountain air.

"The Neuron Institute specializes in one thing," he said. "Fusing man with machine. The story says they've been doing it since Victorian times, right here in the same **spooky** old castle. Some twisted freak called the Baron von Donnerstein started the trend over a hundred years ago. They've gotten much better at it since then."

"I was wrong. It's **Frankenstein**, not

Dracula," Rosie snorted. Then she saw the look on Nedra's face and said, "Oh. Sorry."

"No problem," Nedra said.

But Axel had had the same thought, and he needed to say it out loud.

"That's why they've got my dad, isn't it? They're doing experiments on him. Are they making him into a cyborg?"

"We don't know," Omega said. "And we need to find out."

"But they *could* be, right?"

"I won't lie to you. Your dad might be ... different now. You'd best be ready for anything."

"I don't care!" Nedra said savagely. "I don't care if he's changed into some ... some horrible *machine!* I just want him home where he belongs and that's what's going to happen!"

"Let's focus on the mission," Agent Omega

quickly said. "Castle Donnerstein is in eastern Zamobia, in the forest of Eisenbern. Axel, BEAST, and I will fly there in the MOT-BOL."

Axel was pretty glad about that part. The MOT-BOL might look like a **floating metal jellyfish**, but it was a comfortable way to travel.

"DO WE NEED TO FIGHT?" asked BEAST.

"Fight if you have to, but try to hide as much as you can," said Omega. "Every single person who works for the Institute is a cyborg, with built-in weapons. Then there's the **WarBorgs**, the real heavy hitters, built for the battlefield. So be careful."

"So where are they keeping my dad?" Axel asked.

To be continued ...

READ THEM ALL!